It's Going to be PERFECT!

by Nancy Carlson

PUFFIN BOOKS

To Kari, Kris, and Linda.
Our talk over coffee that snowy morning
gave me the idea for this book.

Also to Kelly.
It's tough being the first child.... But you know what?
It's been perfect! xxoo Mom

PUFFIN BOOKS
Published by the Penguin Group
Penguin Putnam Books for Young Readers, 345 Hudson Street, New York, New York 10014, U.S.A.
Penguin Books Ltd, 27 Wrights Lane, London W8 5TZ, England
Penguin Books Australia Ltd, Ringwood, Victoria, Australia
Penguin Books Canada Ltd, 10 Alcorn Avenue, Toronto, Ontario, Canada M4V 3B2
Penguin Books (N.Z.) Ltd, 182-190 Wairau Road, Auckland 10, New Zealand

Penguin Books Ltd, Registered Offices: Harmondsworth, Middlesex, England

First published in the United States of America by Viking, a member of Penguin Putnam Inc., 1998
Published by Puffin Books, a division of Penguin Putnam Books for Young Readers, 2000

1 3 5 7 9 10 8 6 4 2

Copyright © Nancy Carlson, 1998
All rights reserved

THE LIBRARY OF CONGRESS HAS CATALOGED THE VIKING EDTION AS FOLLOWS:
Carlson, Nancy L.
It's going to be perfect / by Nancy Carlson   p.   cm.
Summary: A mother and her young daughter reflect on the daughter's growing up,
including her infancy, potty training, first words, and starting school.
ISBN 0-670-87802-2 (hc)
[1. Growth—Fiction. 2. Mothers and daughters—Fiction.] I. Title.
PZ7.C21665It 1998 [E]—dc21 97-27689 CIP AC

Puffin Books ISBN 0-14-056723-2

Printed in the United States of America
Set in Pike

Before you were born, I was so excited.
I just knew everything was going to be perfect!

You would sleep through the night.
You would coo and smile at me.

I would know your every need.
This is how I thought we would look.

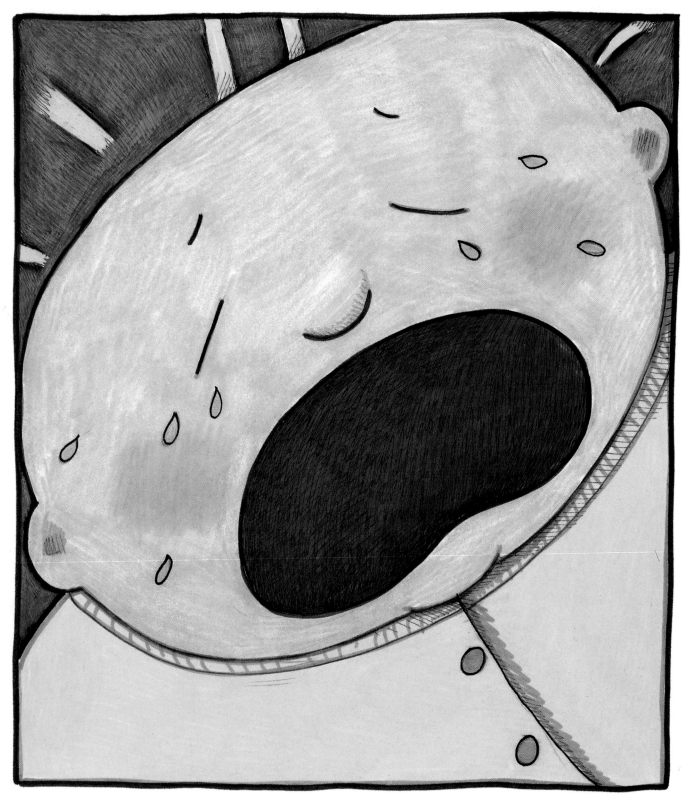

But at first you cried a lot, and you hardly ever slept through the night.

You spit up, and though I tried very hard, I didn't know your every need. This is how we *really* looked after you were born.

But boy am I glad you're here.
You showed me how beautiful 3:00 A.M. can be.

When you were a toddler, I was so excited.
I *knew* everything was going to be perfect.

Potty training would be a breeze,

and I'd teach you to say whole sentences.

But potty training was a challenge for both of us,

and your favorite word was *NO!*

But boy am I glad you're here.
You give me someone to cheer for, and besides . . .

. . . your other favorite word was *Mama!*

When you were three, I was so excited.
I knew everything was going to be perfect.

I would dress you up, and we would go to a restaurant where everyone would admire how neat and polite you were.

But when you were three, the only outfit
you would wear was your cowboy suit,

and we found out that some restaurants don't want kids to have any fun while they're eating.

But boy am I glad you're here.
How else would we have learned how much fun picnics can be?

When you were four, I was so excited.
I just knew everything was going to be perfect.

You would be really eager to start preschool,

and I would relax while you were there.
This is how I thought I would look.

But it wasn't easy saying good-bye
on your first day of school,

and the whole house felt lonely without you in it.
This is how I *really* looked.

But boy am I glad you're here.
If it wasn't for you, our refrigerator would look pretty bare!

When you started kindergarten, I was so excited.
I knew everything was going to be perfect.

I couldn't wait for you to start reading on your own,

except first you had to learn your ABCs like everyone else.

But boy am I glad you're here.
Reading is more fun when we do it together.

Now that you're growing up, I'm so excited because I know
everything is going to be perfect.

It has been so far!